D0568989

ANCIENT WEREWOLVES AND VAMPIRES

The Roots of the Teeth

THE MAKING OF A MONSTER
VAMPIRES & WEREWOLVES

ANCIENT WEREWOLVES AND VAMPIRES
The Roots of the Teeth

by Adelaide Bennett

Mason Crest Publishers

Copyright © 2011 by Mason Crest Publishers. All rights reserved. No part of this publication may be reproduced or transmitted in any form or by any means, electronic or mechanical, including photocopying, recording, taping, or any information storage and retrieval system, without permission from the publisher.

MASON CREST PUBLISHERS INC.
370 Reed Road
Broomall, Pennsylvania 19008
(866)MCP-BOOK (toll free)
www.masoncrest.com

First Printing
9 8 7 6 5 4 3 2 1

ISBN (series) 978-1-4222-1801-3
Paperback ISBN (series) 978-1-4222-1954-6

Library of Congress Cataloging-in-Publication Data

Bennett, Adelaide.
 Ancient werewolves and vampires : the roots of the teeth / by Adelaide Bennett.
      p. cm.
 Includes bibliographical references and index.
 ISBN 978-1-4222-1802-0 (hdbk) ISBN 978-1-4222-1955-3 (pbk.)
 1. Werewolves—Juvenile literature. 2. Vampires—Juvenile literature. I. Title.
 GR830.W4B46 2011
 398.24′54—dc22
                                        2010023796

Produced by Harding House Publishing Service, Inc.
www.hardinghousepages.com
Interior design by MK Bassett-Harvey.
Cover design by Torque Advertising + Design.
Printed in the USA by Bang Printing.

CONTENTS

chapter 1
OUR ANCIENT ANCESTORS' FEARS

Imagine you lived in an early human tribe thousands of years ago. All your life, your people have wandered through the forest, killing deer and rabbits for meat and gathering nuts and roots. Always before, you've had enough food to eat, but this winter has been long and brutal. Your stores of food are gone, and there's nothing else to be found. Even the wild animals are starving.

On a cold, bitter night, you and the others in your tribe huddle around a fire, your stomachs empty and your spirits bleak. An enormous moon rises above the trees, shining its cold light across the snow. Eerie howls drift through darkness, and you shift closer to the man beside you, seeking warmth and comfort. When he turns his head toward you, though, you see he's as frightened as you are. You shudder, with both cold and terror, but finally, you nod off into a shallow sleep.

Something wakes you. The fire has fallen into glowing embers, and the others in your tribe are nothing but dark, huddled shapes, pressed close together against the cold. You hear a twig crack . . . and then a shadow slips from one tree to another beneath the moon's bitter light. Your breath freezes in your chest, and before you can wake the others, the black shape seems to gather itself . . . then leaps—

A scream wakes the rest of the tribe. The blackness has seized one of the tribe's old women by the throat. Before anyone can do anything to save her, she is gone, swallowed by the forest's darkness.

"What was it?" you gasp.

"A wolf," says a woman, but another shakes her head.

"That was no wolf. It was a man. I saw it walk on two legs."

"No, it was a wolf," the first woman insists. She turns to her man. "Go after it. We need to hunt it down and kill it before it attacks us again."

In the moonlight, you see the man's eyes shift away from his woman's gaze. He's afraid, you realize. You're all

Imagine a world where on a cloudy dark night, the only light was a fire: no city lights clouding the sky, no warm glow from streetlights or windows, no electric lights at all (nor even any candles or lamps) anywhere on the planet!

9

afraid. The winter has been too long, too cold, too hungry. There's nowhere safe to hide, and the wild beasts have grown so hungry they'll attack a group of humans around a fire.

In the morning, you will mourn the old woman. But tonight you are all too terrified. The world feels wrong, you think, as though evil has eaten out its heart. Someone builds up the fire again, and you move as close to the warmth and light as you dare.

In the dark night beyond the fire's circle, monsters lurk.

The Darkness Beyond the Fire

In a world like the one we've just described, wolves were humans' enemies. Ancient humans relied on Nature, but they also feared it. Wolves were wily, intelligent creatures that lurked in the darkness and attacked when humans were most vulnerable. No wonder we feared them!

Human beings have always painted their fears with dark colors. Wherever we encounter forces we can neither understand nor control, we tend to see evil and blackness. We project our own deepest terrors outward, onto the world around us. And when we do, a wolf is no longer merely a canine, a relative of the dog that

Paleolithic cave paintings found in France depict a stag standing upright or a man with a stag's head. This figure came to be known as the Horned King, a great were-stag who ruled the Underworld. The Gundestrup cauldron discovered in Denmark (shown here) portrays him as he was typically seen, surrounded by other animals, including a snake. The Horned King may have symbolized humanity's control of nature, allowing humans to live in harmony with wild animals.

has been our best friend down through the millennia. Instead, the wolf is a monster.

An animal that attacks and kills is frightening enough—but it is still just an animal, something that can be out-witted and overcome. But an animal that is part human and part beast is far more horrifying. How can humans hope to overcome something that has the cunning and strength of a beast combined with the intelligence and adaptability of a human?

Werewolves and Vampires: Humanity's Oldest Nightmares

Buffy the Vampire Slayer and Bella in the Twilight series were nowhere near the first humans to encounter these dark creatures. Stone-Age people who lived more than 10,000 years ago already knew and feared the beast who wore a human face and walked with a man's feet. Half-human, half-animal hybrids have slunk through humanity's nightmares for thousands of years.

Researchers know this is true because animal-men have been painted in the world's oldest artwork, the cave paintings of Europe, Africa, and Australia. "We looked at art that goes back to the dawn of humanity and found it had one common feature: animal-human hybrids," said Dr. Christopher Chippindale of Cambridge University's Museum of Archaeology and Anthropology. "Werewolves and vampires are as old as art, in other words. These composite beings, from a world between humans and animals, are a common theme from the beginning of painting."

These half-human monsters have always triggered our deepest and most primitive fears. Perhaps we thought we could control them if we painted them on the walls of caves. Or maybe our long-ago ancestors felt a similar thrill to the one we feel today as we read Anne Rice's vampire stories. The one thing we do know

DID YOU KNOW?

In countries where wolves are unknown, legends tell of tigers who are half human, as well as leopards, hyenas, bears, panthers, snakes, boars, and other animals. Perhaps these stories reflect a universal human uneasiness with our more animal urges, the dark selfish side of our nature that refuses to be tamed. We would like to think of ourselves as superior to the animal world. But are we really?

The ancient Egyptian goddess Sekhmet was half woman and half lion.

from looking at their artwork is that on at least three different continents, across the millennia, humans have shared this common fear.

In Europe, Dr. Chippindale's team found statues of cats with human heads. In Australia, the archeologists discovered paintings of feathered humans with birdlike heads and men with the heads of bats. In one rock painting, one of these animal-headed creatures is attacking a woman.

"Hybrids," Chippindale said, ". . . belong to an imagined world which was powerful, dangerous and—most likely—very frightening." He suspects that primitive people saw these creatures while they were in states of altered consciousness. When they came out of their trances, they painted what they had seen on the cave walls, reminders of what they had experienced, as well as possible triggers that would lead them back into the spirit world.

"The spirit world is a different and separate place, and you need to learn how to access it." Chippindale went on to say:

> They are among the most potent images mankind has ever created. When you enter these caves today, with electric lights and guides, they are still pretty frightening. Armed with only a guttering candle, the experience would have been utterly terrifying in the Stone Age. You would crouch

down a corridor and would then be suddenly confronted by a half-man, half-lion, or something similar.

Why do we humans love to scare ourselves? What Dr. Chippindale describes here is not all that different from going to a modern movie like *Alien* or *Predator*, terrifying ourselves with stories of monsters that are almost human. Something about this ancient image both horrifies us and at the same time stirs our creativity. We are both fascinated and repelled—and we always come back for more.

When it comes to vampires and werewolves, humans have been coming back for more for countless centuries. From the blood-drinking ghouls of Malaysia to the half-cat goddess Sekhmet of ancient Egypt, the bloodthirsty creatures that are neither living nor dead refuse to be laid to rest.

Since the days of antiquity, we humans have loved to scare ourselves with tales of fearsome creatures with glowing red eyes and twisted, distorted shapes, hybrid beasts of evil and darkness.

chapter 2
THE MONSTERS OF MESOPOTAMIA

Nearly eighty centuries ago, Inanna, the Lady of the Sky, went to her garden in Mesopotamia to check on the huluppa tree that had been growing there for ten years. She planned to use the wood to build a new throne, but as she drew near to it, she saw that a serpent had curled around the tree's root, while an owl was raising its young in the tree's branches—and worst of all, Lilith, the evil Wind-Woman, had made her house inside the tree trunk. The Lady of the Sky struck the snake with her staff and killed it. With a screech, the great bird flew away, carrying its young in its talons, and Lilith threw up her hands and ran into the desert.

Lost and lonely, Lilith haunted the shadows between the rocks and hills. People whispered about her, passing

stories of her between them like movie DVDs. She was a lion, they said; she was a storm, said another. She had feet like an owl and huge plumed wings, they agreed. Men could easily fall under her spell, people said, but she could not become pregnant like a normal woman. And worst of all, whispered others, she ate children and women. She was a night demon who drank the blood of pregnant women and killed newborn babies. Sometimes, she would roam the streets like a skinny stray dog, but if you left your door ajar, she would creep into your bedroom and suck the life from you while you slept.

This carving from ancient Babylonia shows a winged woman standing on a lion with owls beside her. The carving, known as the "Queen of the Night," may be one of the earliest portrayals of Lilith.

WHERE AND WHAT WAS MESOPOTAMIA?

The "Land Between the Rivers" lay within the Tigris-Euphrates river system, in what is now modern-day Iraq, as well as some parts of northeastern Syria, southeastern Turkey, and southwestern Iran. Mesopotamia is considered to be the cradle of civilization, and the Sumer, Babylonia, and Assyrian empires all thrived there.

Mesopotamia developed one of the earliest forms of writing and mathematics, and it became a place of learning and culture. Most towns had libraries, and women as well as men learned to read and write. Many Babylonian literary works are still studied today, and one of the most famous of these was the Epic of Gilgamesh, in twelve books. The stories told in this chapter come from these ancient books.

THE BULL-MAN

A hybrid man-beast that was popular in ancient Mesopotamia was known as the sedu, while his female counterpart was the lamassu. Bulls (or sometimes lions) with human heads, these were protective, kind creatures who guarded kings and helped humans fight off the forces of evil.

Blood-Drinking Demons

Lilith was far from being the only vampire-like creature in ancient Mesopotamia. Apparently, the region was crawling with blood-drinking demons. Archeologists have found drawings on pottery shards of hybrid creatures sucking blood from men.

Another Daughter of Heaven, Lamashtu, was a bloodsucker with a lion's head and the body of a donkey. Like

THE FEAR OF CHILDBIRTH

For centuries, childbirth was a bloody and deadly business. Even a hundred years ago, giving birth to a baby could all too easily cost a woman her life. Countless women died in childbirth, and so did their babies. People could not understand or control the mysterious forces that stole mothers and infants from the land of the living—and so they made up stories to explain these fearful and tragic events.

Lilith, she preyed mostly on newborns and their mothers, hovering around pregnant women as they went into labor, so she could be ready to snatch the babies and eat them. An ancient text describes Lamashtu: "Wherever she comes, wherever she appears, she brings evil and destruction. Men, beasts, trees, rivers, roads, buildings, she brings harm to them all. A flesh-eating, blood-sucking monster is she."

Seven evil spirits also haunted Mesopotamia. According to the ancient writing,

> *Seven are they! Seven are they!*
> *Spirits that diminish the heaven and earth,*
> *That diminish the land,*
> *Of giant strength, and giant tread,*
> *Demons like raging bulls, great ghosts,*
> *Ghosts that break through all houses,*
> *Demons that have no shame,*
> *Seven are they!*
> *Knowing no care, they grind the land like corn;*
> *Knowing no mercy, they rage against mankind,*
> *They spill man's blood like rain,*
> *Devouring his flesh and sucking his veins.*
> *Demons of wickedness, ceaselessly devouring blood.*

Hungry Ghosts

Dying in ancient Mesopotamia was risky business. If your family did not prepare your body properly for the afterlife, or if through some misfortune you died alone, you could end up in a very bad neighborhood of the underworld. There, the only thing for you to eat would be the cold, dark dirt. Understandably, you would be hungry—and you would want to find a way to escape your new bleak residence.

Luckily (or not!), the dead could sometimes return to the land of the living, but not in their old shapes. Especially at certain times of the year, the dead could

During the Renaissance, Christians sometimes confused Lilith with the
serpent in the Garden of Eden (as shown to the left in this painting by
Michelangelo), and they blamed her for Adam and Eve's downfall. By
the nineteenth century, Lilith's image had become far more romantic and
beautiful, as in this painting by Dante Gabriel Rossetti.

creep through the gates of the underworld and once more walk among the living as cold, bloodless forms. To prolong their stay in the over-world, they would drink the blood of living victims.

The Gidim were a particular kind of hungry ghost who could not enter the land of the dead for one reason or another. They might have had no gifts to offer the gatekeepers—or their hatred for a person who was still living might have tied them to this world. In any case, they did not consume actual flesh, but instead they were walking shadows who could suck the life force from a person, leaving only bruises on his neck. They could also enter a person's ear and possess her (which was a good reason to wear charmed earrings if you were going to wander around Mesopotamia at night).

Not all Gidim were unfriendly, though. In the Month of Ghosts (what we call August), they could return to the land of the living to visit their loved ones, who welcomed them with festivals. Good Gidim would then slip away to their place in the underworld—but the evil ones would linger among the living, sucking on their spiritual blood, drawing out the essence of their lives.

Passing the Stories Along

The echoes of these stories spread to other regions in the ancient world. Lilith traveled as far as the Garden of

Eden, where eventually (according to both Jewish and some Christian traditions), she was said to be Adam's first wife. Other variations of blood-sucking demons and hungry ghosts also showed up in ancient Greece and then Rome.

Were these stories passed along like a game of gossip, whispered from ear to ear around firesides?

Or did the creatures themselves swoop on dark wings across the Mediterranean?

chapter 3
THE GRUESOME CREATURES OF ANCIENT GREECE

Long ago in the sunny land of Greece, people sang and laughed as they toiled the earth by day—but at night, strange footsteps were heard across the land: THUD-click, THUD-click, THUD-click. When the sound echoed down the streets or along the roads, people made sure their doors were barred and their fires built high. They knew that Empusa was passing by.

Empusa had hair like flames, a face like a goddess, and a voice as shrill as a thousand mosquitoes. She had been born with only one leg—a donkey's leg—but she wore a bronze prosthetic leg on the other side, so she could wander the roads, looking for travelers to devour. Female travelers were gone in a gulp, but Empusa fancied the men. She would lure them to her bed, where she would suck their blood while they slept.

As the centuries went by, however, Empusa grew old. She shriveled and grew small. Eventually, she was only a whispered memory. For the rest of time, she wandered the hills, a shape-shifter who could appear as a dog, an ox, or a mule. Her only pastime now was pestering shepherds watching their sheep at night. Once a terrifying female vampire, she had faded away into little more than a small, annoying were-creature.

Lamia

Like Empusa, Lamia started out her life beautiful and powerful. She was a princess, the daughter of King Belus of Egypt and the granddaughter of the god Poseidon. When her father died, Lamia became queen of one of his territories, the land of Libya. She held court there, traveled, dallied with men. And eventually, she caught the eye of the highest of the gods, Zeus himself.

Lamia and Zeus's love affair was long, and she gave birth to several of his children. Eventually, however, his wife found out. Hera was furious at her husband's infidelity (though you would think she would have been used to it by now, since Zeus apparently could resist no one with ovaries). In a jealous rage, Hera killed Lamia's children.

Lamia's grief drove her insane. She stopped washing. She no longer wore her beautiful clothes or combed her hair. Instead, she haunted the streets at night,

Lamia could take out her eyeballs whenever she liked, but she could still not escape the vision of her lost children that haunted her. In the end, she was a snake that craved the blood of children.

THE LITERARY LAMIA

The ancient Greek poet Horace wrote about Lamia, and she has continued to interest writers and artists down through the centuries. New stories grew up around her in the process. The nineteenth-century poet John Keats was particularly interested in her, and romantic artists of the 1800s liked to portray the once-hideous monster as a beautiful and tragic woman. The artist John William Waterhouse created this painting of Lamia in 1905.

PARALLELS ON THE OTHER SIDE OF THE WORLD

In Mexico still today, the nights are sometimes haunted by a woman's sobs: La Llorona, the Weeping Woman. La Llorona's children died as a result of her lover's faithlessness, and driven insane with sorrow, she still wanders Mexico's dark streets, luring disobedient children and faithless men to their deaths. Anthropologists suspect that La Llorona's stories were born hundreds of years ago, when the ancient Aztecs told similar stories about the goddess Cihuacoatl, the Snake Woman with the head of a skull who helped create humanity from the blood and ground bones of her enemies.

listening outside the doors for the cries of other children. The sound of children's voices both drew her, and at the same time, made her weep with sorrow and rage. She was filled with a terrible emptiness, a hunger. One dark night, she crept through the window of a house where a child was crying—and she ate him.

After that, Lamia's hunger for children was insatiable. The more she ate, the more hideous she grew. She could no longer close her eyes in sleep. Instead, her eyes were constantly open, staring at the vision of her dead children. There was no escape from her torment. Zeus, feeling sad and guilty, tried to help his former lover by giving her the ability to remove her eyeballs and drop them into her pocket.

His efforts were too little too late. The once-beautiful Lamia was a monster now, with the scaly tale of an enormous snake. She slithered through the darkness, a filthy, bloated serpent. As the years went by, she grew stupid. She no longer remembered she was a king's daughter, the granddaughter of a god. Now she was nothing but an empty gullet, a gaping mouth, a desperate hunger for blood and flesh.

The Stryx

The Greeks apparently had their issues with women, for many of their monsters were female. The stryx—also known as the striges—like Lamia,

Vampires in the Odyssey?

One of the most famous of ancient Greek tales is Homer's epic Odyssey. In it, Homer tells of the undead, shadowy beings too unsubstantial to make their voices heard by the living. The only way they could gain enough strength to communicate was by first drinking blood.

Kirghiz avec un aigle

ODYSSEUS AND THE CROW-WOMEN

Homer also describes Odysseus's encounter with creatures that sound very like the stryx, bloodthirsty crow-women who lured sailors to their deaths. This painting by John William Waterhouse shows Odysseus and his men trying to resist the lures of the siren by covering their ears and tying themselves to the ship.

THE BLOODTHIRSTY BRIDE

Both the ancient Greeks and Romans told the tale of a young man named Menippus who married a beautiful young woman. At the wedding, one of the guests, a noted philosopher named Apollonius of Tyana, grew suspicious of the bride. He observed her carefully, and finally, he accused her of being a vampire. The bride immediately confessed her true nature. She had wanted to marry Menippus merely to have him around as a handy source of fresh blood.

feasted on children, and like Empusa, they preyed on hapless young men. They preened their black crow feathers over their breasts and screamed into the darkness, harbingers of war and disaster.

The ancient Greek poets Horace, Seneca, and Ovid all wrote of these bloodthirsty bird-women. Their fame spread to ancient Rome, and there they turned into the Strigoi, the earliest versions of the vampires we know and love today.

These primitive vampires lingered in the darkness, down through the centuries. Their stories spread throughout Europe, and eventually, they would take deep root in Eastern Europe, especially in the thick, dark forests of Transylvania. But in the meantime, other bloodsucking creatures were haunting the nightmares of humans who lived in the lands to the east of Europe. These monsters were different—and yet chillingly the same.

The First Werewolf?

Another famous Greek poet, Ovid, told the tale of King Lycaon who was punished for serving the flesh of a dismembered child as a meal to the gods. The angry gods turned the king into a wolf.

chapter 4
THE SPIRITS OF THE FAR EAST

The ancient Chinese believed that humans had two souls. The Hun was the superior soul, the good spirit, the best of the person. If a person died, and her Hun appeared to her friends and family, it would look the same as she had in life, but in spirit form. The other part of a human being, however, was the P'o, the inferior soul, the evil spirit, all that was selfish and brutal in a person. The P'o remained in the body after death and was buried. Sometimes, though, if it were strong enough, it could prevent decomposition. It could even make the dead body get up and walk and talk.

The Ch'iang Shih were a special and terrible kind of P'o, a demon that could inhabit any dead body, not just its own. It could even create a new being from a few broken bones and scraps of rotted flesh. The Ch'iang Shih haunted the night, their red eyes glowing in the darkness, their damp, moldy odor warning travelers they were near. Their long fingernails were as sharp as vulture's talons, and hair the color of pale green mold grew on their bodies. If they snatched an unwary traveler along a dark road, they would first suck out his blood. When he was dead and white, they would go on to their second course and devour his bloodless flesh.

Japan's Vampire Were-Cat

Across the sea from China, Japan had its own share of demons and evil spirits. One of the most insidious was a shape-shifting vampire cat that sucked the lifeblood from its victim, then buried the body and took the victim's shape as its own. It would go on next to prey upon the victim's unsuspecting loved ones.

Kirghiz avec un aigle

The Langsuir

A beautiful woman in a flowing green robe drifted through the warm dark nights of ancient Malaysia. Her black hair fell to her ankles, and her fingernails were as sharp as broken glass. After giving birth to a still-born baby, the Langsuir had gone mad with grief. She escaped into the jungle, where as the years went by, she turned into a demon. She could easily have been a sister of the Greek Lamia—except for the deep bloody hole at the back of her neck. The Langsuir killed other women's babies—like Lamia—but then she pressed their bodies to the hole in her neck, so that their blood could flow into her.

The Langsuir started out as a single woman with a particular appearance. She was so feared, however, that the Malaysians began to suspect that a single demon could not be in as many places as she was rumored to be. A langsuir could also be created, they realized, if a woman died during childbirth. She would turn into an owl-woman, stealing fish from the fishermen when she could not get the human flesh she now craved.

To prevent this terrible transformation, the ancient Malaysians filled the dead woman's mouth with glass beads, they put eggs in her armpits, and thrust needles into the palms of her hands. If they failed to do this and the woman became a langsuir, they would have to capture her, carefully following the proper procedures once they had her. Her nails and hair would need to be cut, and then the hair and clippings stuffed into the hole at the back of her neck. This would allow her to go back to her life, behaving like a normal woman, so long as the hole in her neck remained plugged.

Other Malaysian Vampire Women

The Pennanggalan, like the langsuir, preferred the blood of young children, but she was an old and ugly woman. Her appearance became even more startlingly hideous one day when a passerby startled her so badly that she kicked herself under the chin, separating her head from her body. The head flew up into the treetops, a gory trail of intestines hanging from the stump of the neck.

Pennanggalan might have been condemned to hang out in the tree for all eternity, but a helpful monster happened past and taught her the knack of stuffing her intestines back into her body and reattaching her head. She could then remove it again as the fancy took her. In her body-less form, she was prone to feasting on human flesh, and the unsuspecting traveler needed to be careful to search the treetops for her head with its dangling intestines. Even if he escaped being turned into her next meal, a drop of her blood falling down on him as he passed beneath her tree could make oozing sores appear on his skin, and he would likely die from a hideous disease.

Like so many of these nasty women, the Pennanggalan's preferred meal was newborn flesh. The Pennanggalan's intestines would often become so bloated with the blood of her victims that she would have to soak them in a vat of vinegar to shrink them down enough to fit back inside her body. To protect their babies, the ancient Malaysians strung thorns around their windows and doors to snag her dangling intestines and trap her.

Tiny Vampires

Ancient Malaysia was a scary place. Not only did you need to avoid the bloodthirsty women who haunted the night, but you could all too easily fall victim to the polong, an inch-long humanoid with a craving for human blood.

The polong hangs out with another small friend, the pelesit. The pelesit has a whip-like tail with a sharp tip

ONE MORE MALAYSIAN VAMPIRE DEMON

The bajang, a bloodthirsty demon, usually looked like a large lizard or a weasel-like creature. A sorcerer made this demon from the soul of an infant that died at birth and was freshly buried. Like the polong, bajangs were used to harm enemies, who were seized by convulsions and fainting spells after they had been bitten by a bajang. If the creator was discovered and killed, the bajang would also be destroyed.

that's perfect for boring a hole in human flesh. Once the hole is big enough, the pelesit chirps like a cricket, its signal to its friend that it's time for supper. The polong enters the body of the unfortunate victim and feasts. The victim begins to have nightmares of evil cats, and eventually he goes insane.

These two tiny evil friends are created by witchcraft. The polong is made from the blood of a murdered man. It serves the sorcerer who made it and obeys its

The Vetala was a frightening fellow, one of the worst of India's vampire-like creatures.

master's orders. (Its creator will nourish it with drops of his own blood until he is ready to release it to attack an enemy.) The pelesit, meanwhile, was made from the tongue of a dead baby.

The Demons of India

Ancient India had its share of vampire-like creatures as well. The warm humid nights were filled with terrors and the terrible hungers of the living dead. The Pishacha, the returned spirits of evildoers or those who had died insane, lurked in the darkness, waiting for human flesh. The BrahmarākŚhasa terrified the inhabitants of northern India by carrying a skull from which it drank blood, while its head was encircled by a wreath of intestines.

And the Rakshasa had deadly talons and long, gleaming eyes like slits. Their skin was yellow, green, or blue, and their faces were deformed. The Rakshasa haunted graveyards, where they would sometimes animate the dead bodies and walk disguised among the living. If you had the misfortune to be scratched by a Rakshasa, you would suffer a painful and hideous death. Worse yet, the Rakshasa had a taste for human flesh (though they could be contented by eating horses instead). Sometimes, however, despite their evil natures, the Rakshasa took a liking to a particular human, whom they would then endow with endless riches.

Like the Rakshasa, the Vetala also lurked in burial grounds and could animate corpses. They had voracious appetites and would tear their human prey to shreds. In the daytime, they could be spotted hanging upside down in trees, their leathery wings folded like bats. This demon, like the Rakshasa, occasionally had a kindly side to its nature and would help humans in distress.

In India, Hinduism has long recognized that things are seldom black and white. Destructive demons can be moved by compassion, and even death has a creative aspect. The Goddess Kali is the embodiment of this thought.

Ancient Literature

Tales of India's vampire-like creatures are written in the Sanskrit language, in books that were written thousands of years ago. Some of these stories appear in the Vedas, which were written around 1500 BCE.

India's Goddess of Destruction

On a day long, long ago, Mother Durga, the self-sufficient one, she who is patient and invincible, whose compassion is fierce and unfailing, was in battle with the demon

जय महाकाली मा

The goddess Kali dancing on her husband's body after her battle with the blood-seed demon.

HINDUISM

Hinduism, one of the world's great religions, was born in India thousands of years ago. It is the world's oldest living religions, and today, it is also the world's third-largest religion (after Christianity and Islam), with about one billion people around the world who consider themselves to be Hindus.

Hinduism varies greatly from region to region (and even person to person). Its ancient scriptures (written down between 1100 and 1700 BCE from stories and wisdom that had been handed down orally for countless centuries before that) tell the tales of many gods and goddesses (like Kali and her husband Shiva). In some ways, however, these gods and goddesses are all simply aspects of the one Supreme Spirit. Some Hindus see this as the Divine Principle, but others believe in a personal God, a Supreme Being.

Raktabija (which means "Blood Seed"). No matter how hard she and her warrior women fought, they could not destroy him, for each time a drop of his blood fell on the ground, it sprang up as the demon's clone, fighting at his side. Soon the battlefield was crowded with the demon's duplicates, and Durga and her warriors were forced to fall back.

Just as things looked hopeless, the Goddess Kali sprang forth from Durga's frowning face, her four arms waving weapons. Bearing her skull-topped staff and clad in a tiger's skin, she opened her mouth wide and roared at Raktabija. As she leapt upon him, the necklace of skulls that hung round her neck clattered and bounced on her breasts, and her red eyes blazed. She sucked the last drop of blood from the demon's body, and then she stuffed his clones into her mouth. With the bodies hanging between her long, sharp teeth, she danced in victory and rage across the bloody battlefield.

Lost in the sheer joy of her victory, she grew wilder and wilder, her feet stamping the earth until the world itself began to sway and tremble. Her husband, Lord Shiva himself, took her by the arms and asked her to stop before she destroyed the world, but she was too drunk with joy to listen. Then Shiva lay down like a corpse among the dead bodies that littered the battlefield. Even now, Kali failed to notice her husband's presence, and her feet stamped in rage across his body. He absorbed the shock of her dance into his own body, and now at last, Kali came to her senses. When she realized

THE GODDESS SEKHMET

Far from ancient India, in the equally ancient land of Egypt, the Goddess Sekhmet shared many of Kali's qualities. Like Kali, she was the goddess of both destruction and creation, the Great Mother as well as the Lady of Dread. She was the Avenger of Wrongs and the Scarlet Lady, who dressed herself in a robe of blood. She was the bringer of disease—and the one who cured all diseases.

Unlike Kali, however, Sekhmet, was also a were-creature. She had a woman's body with the head of a lion. Her thirst for blood was terrible and unending; at the end of a battle, like Kali, she could often not control her lust for blood, and she would turn from her enemies to her human worshippers. Her destructive urges sometimes brought salvation, however: the Nile River was said to turn to blood when it flooded (carrying the red silt from upriver), and Sekhmet would gulp it down, thus saving humanity.

she had stepped on her husband, her head hung and she bit her tongue in shame.

Death and Life

Kali's worshippers knew they must face her curse, the terror of death, as willingly as they accepted her blessings. For them, wisdom meant learning that no coin has only one side: death cannot exist without life, and life cannot exist without death. By acknowledging this as it was portrayed in this story of Kali and Shiva, many Hindus believed a state of peace could be reached even within life's chaos.

Kali was clearly far more than any vampire, and despite her fearsome appearance, she is still worshipped and loved in much of India. Her name means "The Black One," "Time," "Death," and "Beyond Time." She is the destroyer—but she is also the redeemer and creator. Out of destruction, she brings new life.

Kali embodies our human fascination with death—as well as our race's most primitive belief that death is not the final end of life. Kali's place in the Hindu pantheon of gods acknowledges that life is full of change, that nothing lasts forever, that death cannot be escaped. At the same time, however, those who worship Kali rejoice in the knowledge that even death is full of the invincible creative spirit that lies at the heart of reality.

Humans have feared for their babies since the dawn of time. For hundreds of years, most children died before they were five years old. Tales of vampires helped explain and make sense of this tragedy.

Our Darkest Fears

In some small way, our fascination with vampires and werewolves expresses this same concept. Millennia ago, our ancestors faced their worst fears—the fear of death, the fear of darkness, the fear of childbirth, the fear of nature itself—and they turned their fears into creatures with faces, into stories. These stories sent shivers up and down their spines (just as many of our novels of vampires and werewolves do today), but they also delighted them (just as our horror films still do). Human creativity gives the darkness shape.

The Vampire God of Nepal

Ancient paintings on the walls of caves in Nepal depict blood-drinking creatures, including the "Lord of Death," who is depicted holding a blood-filled goblet in the form of a human skull while he stands in a pool of blood. Some of these wall paintings are as old as 3000 BCE.

Vampires and werewolves have terrified humans down through the centuries. And at the same time, they have always fascinated us as well. These hybrid creatures, both human and beast, with their terrible thirst for blood, represent the darkness. This darkness lies both within the human heart and beyond it, in the mysterious night. Will we ever conquer it?

Do we even want to?

WORDS YOU MAY NOT KNOW

adaptability: The ability to change to deal with different circumstances.

altered consciousness: The states in which people experience the world through their senses differently than they usually do. Altered states of consciousness can be caused by illness or certain drugs, for example, or can refer to dream states.

avenger: A person who punishes another for their actions, on behalf of a person they have wronged.

chaos: Confusion and disorder.

composite: Something that is made up of different kinds of things.

dread: Great fear or horror.

embodies: Gives a physical form to something, such as an idea or concept, for example.

hybrid: Something made up of two or more different species or kinds of things.

insatiable: Unable to be satisfied.

invincible: Not able to be harmed or conquered.

millennia: Thousands of years.

pantheon: The group of all gods in a particular mythology or tradition.

potent: Powerful.

primitive: Having to do with early history or the early version of something.

project: To give something outside yourself credit for causing feelings or attitudes that really come from within yourself.

redeemer: Someone who saves one or more people by paying their debts or ransom.

repelled: Horrified or disgusted by something; wanting to have nothing to do with something.

salvation: The act of saving someone or something, protecting it or taking it out of harm's way.

shards: Broken pieces.

trances: States of altered consciousness in which people are between waking and sleeping and in a semiconscious daze. In some belief systems, trances are the states in which a person is controlled by an outside force or spirit or receives wisdom from a god or other spiritual being.

wily: Sneaky, tricky, and deceitful.

Find Out More on the Internet

Ancient Vampires in Folklore
www.lesvampires.org/mirrorsportal/ancient.html

Chiang-shih
www.deliriumsrealm.com/delirium/articleview.asp?Post=17

Empusa and Lamiae: Vampires, Demons, and Monsters in Greek Legend
www.theoi.com/Phasma/Empousai.html

Goddess Sekhmet, An Ancient Egyptian Vampire?
www.vampirenerd.com/2009/08/goddess-sekhmet-ancient-egyptian.html

Kali: The Dark Mother
hinduism.about.com/od/hindugoddesses/a/makali.htm

The Lilith Page, on Jewish and Christian Literature
jewishchristianlit.com//Topics/Lilith/

Mount Lykaion's Curse
www.werewolves.com/mount-lykaions-curse/

Sweet Penina: The Tale of the Penanggalan
www.agonyagogo.com/penina.html

Further Reading

Baring-Gould, Sabine. *The Book of Werewolves.* Charlotte, N.C.: IAP, 2009.

Greer, John Michael. *Monsters: An Investigator's Guide to Magical Beings.* St. Paul, Minn.: Llewellyn Press, 2001.

Lim, Danny. *The Malaysian Book of the Undead.* Petaling Jaya, Malaysia: Matahari Books, 2008.

Maberry, Jonathan, and David F. Kramer. *They Bite!: Endless Cravings of Supernatural Predators.* New York: Kensington, 2009.

Murgatroyd, Paul. *Mythical Monsters in Classical Literature.* London: Duckworth, 2007.

Śivadāsa. *The Five-and-Twenty Tales of the Genie.* Trans. by Chandra Rajan. New York: Penguin Classics, 2006.

Thompson, R. Campbell. *The Devils and Evil Spirits of Babylonia: Being Babylonian and Assyrian Incantations Against the Demons, Ghouls, Vampires, Hobgoblins, Ghosts, and Kindred Evil Spirits, Which Attack Mankind.* Charleston, S.C.: Forgotten Books, 2010.

Bibliography

"Greek Vampires." vampires.monstrous.com/greek_vampires.htm (1 May 2010).

"Kali, the Dark Mother." hinduism.about.com/od/hindugoddesses/a/ma (5 June 2010).

"Lamia, a Greek Vampire Legend." www.vampiretruth.com/lamia-a- (4 June 2010).

Spence, Lewis. *Myths and Legends of Babylonia and Assyria*. London, UK: G. G. Harrap, 1928.

"Study of the Greek Vrykolakas." bylightunseen.net/vrykolak.htm (1 May 2010).

Summers, Montague. *The Vampire: His Kith and Kin*. New Hyde Park, N.Y.: University Books, 1960.

Thompson, E. Campbell. *The Devils and Evil Spirits of Babylonia*. London, UK: Luzac, 1903-04.

_____. *Semitic Magic: Its Origin and Development*. London, UK: Luzac, 1908.

"Vampires in Ancient Babylonia and Assyria." www.answers.com/topic/vampires-in-ancient-babylon-and-assyria (30 April 2010).

Index

Picture Credits

Creative Commons: pp. 10, 11, 18, 20, 23, 25, 26, 30, 34, 37, 40, 48
Dahl, Jeff: p. 54
Dover: pp. 21, 46
Heys, Ben; Fotolia: p. 44
Korzh, Yegor; Fotolia: p. 9
Kraft, Ralf; Fotolia: pp. 16, 56
Lagutin, Pavel; Fotolia: p. 33
National Museum, Copenhagen: p. 51
Photosani, Fotolia: p. 6

ABOUT THE AUTHOR

The 1970s Gothic soap opera *Dark Shadows* had a forma-
tive influence on Adelaide Bennett when she was growing up. She continues to be interested in the darker
side of the supernatural world, and enjoys reading and
studying the history, psychology, and mythology that
is interwoven with stories of the supernatural. With
degrees in both psychology and writing, she enjoys the
opportunity to write about topics that combined her
two fields of interest.